To all the moms for all that they do

PARK
½ MILE

Toad on the Road: Mama and Me
Copyright © 2018 by Stephen Shaskan
All rights reserved. Manufactured in China.
No part of this book may be used or reproduced in any manner whatsoever without
written permission except in the case of brief quotations embodied in critical articles and
reviews. For information address HarperCollins Children's Books, a division of HarperCollins
Publishers, 195 Broadway, New York, NY 10007.
www.harpercollinschildrens.com

ISBN 978-0-06-239349-4

The artist used Photoshop to create the digital illustrations for this book.
18 19 20 21 22   SCP   10 9 8 7 6 5 4 3 2 1

❖
 First Edition

TOAD on the ROAD
Mama and Me

STEPHEN SHASKAN

HARPER

An Imprint of HarperCollinsPublishers

Mama and Toad out on the road.
Go, Mama, go! Go, little toad!

Why, who's that friend
around the bend?

Alas! Alas!
It's a . . .

Mama and Toad will save the day!

Everyone shout: Hip hip hooray!

Thanks, little bud, and Mama Toad, too.
If you weren't here, what would I do?

With gas in my truck and good friends like you,
my delivery will surely get through.

Mama and Toad out on the road.
Go, Mama, go! Go, little toad!

Why, who's that friend
around the bend?

Oh drat! Oh drat!
It's a . . .

Mama and Toad will save the day!
Everyone shout: Hip hip hooray!

Thanks, little guy, and Mama Toad, too.
If you weren't here, what would I do?

With this new tire and good friends like you,
my delivery will surely get through.

Mama and Toad out on the road.
Go, Mama, go! Go, little toad!

Mama and Toad will save the day!

Everyone shout: Hip hip hooray!

VROOM!
VROOM!
VROOM!

Thanks, little pal, and Mama Toad, too.
If you weren't here, what would I do?

With my car unstuck and good friends like you,
my delivery will surely get through.

Mama and Toad out on the road.
Go, Mama, go! Go, little toad!

See all those friends
around the bend?

It's a party and everyone's here—
a bounce house, balloons, and pizza to share!

Thanks, little toad, and Mama Toad, too.

Hooray to our friends for all that they do!